PRAISE FOR THE WRITING
OF MATTHEW CHENEY

I0555641

Changes in the La

"The final page gave me goosebumps—a beautifully written piece of New England horror."
—ELIZABETH HAND, author of *A Haunting on the Hill*

"Bloody good folk horror. Cheney's writing is sublime."
—LAIRD BARRON, author of *Not a Speck of Light*

"Who knew nature could be so terrifying? Horror fans with a healthy respect for our environment are going to love this novella."
—*Independent Book Review*

"It's powerful, it's visceral, and most of all, it's so damn smart. But then, I wouldn't expect less from Matthew Cheney."
—IAN MOND for *Locus Magazine*

The Last Vanishing Man

"*The Last Vanishing Man* is first-rate! I can't—as they say—recommend it highly enough."
—SAMUEL R. DELANY, Four-time Nebula Award, two-time Hugo Award, winning author and Science Fiction Hall of Fame inductee

"Weird, dark, and wonderful visions and hallucinations from a wholly unique voice."
—JEFFREY FORD, author of *A Natural History of Hell*

"There is a genuine beauty in Cheney's clear-eyed prose, which immerses you in his world, even if the subject matter is challenging."
—IAN MOND for *Locus Magazine*

Blood: Stories

"Rooted in a sense of place, but yearning for a world beyond, the stories in *Blood* chart heartbreak, solitude, and adventure in equal measure. It's rare to read fiction with such depth that's also so entertaining. One of my favorite reads of the past year."
—JEFF VANDERMEER, author of the Southern Reach Trilogy

"Matthew Cheney has long been one of the most astute and eloquent presences on the literary web, and now he reveals himself to be a fiction writer of equally high abilities. Some of the stories in *Blood* are informed by science fiction or fantasy, some by literary criticism, some by postmodern experimentation, and all of them by his own keen intellect, adventurous hand, and broad yet exacting sympathy."
—KEVIN BROCKMEIER, author of *The Brief History of the Dead*

CHANGES
IN THE
LAND

Also by Matthew Cheney

––––––––––––

The Last Vanishing Man and Other Stories

Blood: Stories

CHANGES
IN THE
LAND

MATTHEW CHENEY

LETHE

Published in 2024 by Lethe Press
www.lethepressbooks.com • lethepress@aol.com

Cover design and layout by JeremyJohnParker.com

ISBN: 978-1-59021-526-5

for Richard Scott Larson

Throughout his life, Elias Thornton has suffered a recurring nightmare:

He dreams himself at twilight, walking through shadows that soon reveal him to be approaching a grove of swollen maple trees around an old well made of stone, impossibly deep and dark. Dogs wail in the distance. Crimson deer run through the woods. From the depths of the well rises a sharp sound, a baby's cry. He kneels at the well and squints and tries to see through the dark, but he sees only birds down in the well, crows perhaps, a mass of them, feathers fluttering, wings flapping, beaks pecking hysterically at each other's eyes. Vines crawl around his ankles and up his legs, wrap around his torso, lifting him and strangling him, holding him over the well — and always in the dream, at this point, he looks down and sees that the well is an opening filled with clear winter sky, starlit and glimmering, and he reaches an arm out toward the sky, but he cannot touch anything, cannot reach anything, because the vines are barbed, they tear into his skin, they twist his neck, they slice his lips and pull out his teeth. He wants to scream, wants the sky to hear him and welcome him, but he cannot scream because his mouth is full of broken teeth and shredded flesh and blood.

The dream regularly pursued his nights when he was a young man, causing him to wake sometimes choking and screaming.

Those nights terrified his wife, Charlotte. She learned to talk him through it, though, to help him quiet himself and rest and even sleep again. For quite a few years, he did not have the dream. Then, when Josiah and Drusilla were teenagers, two or three years after Charlotte's death, the dream returned. He entered its familiar terror every few months thereafter.

Now and then, he wonders what Valeria Adams dreams about. In all their decades of knowing each other, she has never, that he can recall, even once spoken of a dream.

Excerpts from the first (and only) report by Dr. Steven A. Baird to the Hoadley Foundation, September 2017, courtesy Milne Special Collections and Archives, Dimond Library, University of New Hampshire:

Having presented the above information gleaned from six months of research at small-town libraries and historical societies (in addition to years of earlier research in major archives and collections of public records), I hope you will forgive the personal tone henceforward as I bring the information together. My own story has become meaningful to this research and will move the scattered and, frankly, unsatisfying report above toward a more promising conclusion — a conclusion that points the way toward truly exciting new opportunities during the second half of this generous grant. I apologize for some repetitions of information from above; it seems necessary for the sake of context.

Ancestry has never interested me. This may seem a strange statement for a professor of history to make, as one might assume someone who has devoted his life to the excavation and explication of the past would be fascinated by lineage, but my scholarship has always tended toward systems more than individuals, environments more than people. Family, in particular, is a topic I have not only ignored but avoided. I have no siblings; I barely knew any of my grandparents or other relatives; my father died when I was a child, and my mother when I was in college. Scholarship became a refuge from the family tree. Asked about home, I might deflect by musing on the insights available from research comparing the movement of water — natural, municipal, commercial — in New York, Texas, and North Dakota over the last four centuries. Faced with questions about whether I plan to marry, I can cite interesting facts about how certain marriage practices correlate with practices throughout the history of agriculture. Pressed to share my thoughts on children, I may note how many cultures have practiced infanticide.

Thus, I believed for most of my career that my persistent interest in Adams Park derived from some connection to the other subjects of my research, though I struggled to say exactly what that connection might be. Still, all my best scholarship originated from intuition, often following extended periods of more-or-less directionless research. I held onto the idea of Adams Park even though I could not put my finger on the significance of the place to my work. Long before I ever set foot near the grounds, I knew that *something* about the park was relevant to my interests, and in spare moments in the library, I would find myself, sometimes with barely a conscious intention, scouring old newspapers and books for any mention of its name. I assumed my curiosity stemmed from those few and often mysterious mentions. The origin of that curiosity, however, was something I never reflected on and, at the time, barely remembered: a postcard found in a shoebox in my mother's closet after her death. The postcard rested alongside some old letters to people whose names I did not recognize, a long-neglected address book with only a smattering of addresses scrawled in its pages (more names I didn't recognize), and a handful of pictures of my toddler self. The handwriting on the postcard was hard to make out, the message unmemorable, but I was amazed to see what looked like a scene from an African safari with the location given as the town of Colton, New Hampshire.

Colton, I soon learned, is a village in northwestern New Hampshire.[1] It shares the many acres of Adams Park with four neighbors, but what distinguishes Colton is that it is the home of the central gate to the park. The gate is not ostentatious. In old postcards, it is little more than a few wood beams; more recently, it has been replaced with a steel gate of the kind used by high-security government facilities, complete with security cameras on either side. Over the years, the many miles of fencing around the park have been replaced and upgraded when bison, elk, and (especially) wild pigs found their way through weaker sections and wreaked havoc with people's gardens. The annoyance at escaped animals has occasionally led to calls for the park to be regulated, and the few newspaper articles about such events provided the only confirmation I could find of the park's con-

---

1. Colton is roughly 31 square miles in size, with an official population of 339 people in the most recent census, which is slightly higher than past censuses.

tinued existence after the deaths in 1931 of **Claudius Adams** (b. 1908) and his father, **Tiberius Franklin Adams** (b. 1873) in what was reported as a hunting accident on the grounds.[2]

Though the park had been built as a private game reserve for hunting and hosted all the famed hunting men of the day (including Theodore Roosevelt), after 1931, record of such use disappears. All information about the family dries up at that time as well.

———————

———————

2. Though I have considered most of the early history of the family and Adams Park to be irrelevant to this report, it is worth noting that the first decades of the park are somewhat better documented than anything later, a consequence of the prestige of the industrialist Alexander Adams (1825-1864) and his son Augustus (born Geoffrey, 1847-1895). The family had long owned significant amounts of land throughout the northeastern United States, and Augustus was able to purchase more quite easily as westward migration and the ravages of the Civil War together put much real estate on the market at low prices. An 1867 state law mandated sale of all of New Hampshire's public lands; that combined with many farmers abandoning their property to go out west made acquisition of large tracts inexpensive. Thus was Augustus able to gather the land that would come to be known as Adams Park. The family's Adams & Sons timber juggernaut, like other timber interests, acquired massive areas at this time as well, though there is no evidence that Adams & Sons had anything to do with the park, which was strictly private and controlled by Augustus alone. As would other timber businesses, Adams & Sons contributed to the massive deforestation of northern New Hampshire in the later 19th century, while Adams Park would remain a strange haven amidst the destruction, itself only threatened by the great forest fire of 1903 (likely caused by irresponsible logging). While the majority of the game at the park always seem to have been moose, bison, deer, elk, antelope, caribou, and wild pigs, by the 1870s there are various customs and health records for a handful of particularly exotic animals: Himalayan mountain goats, giraffes and zebras from Africa, and two elephants from Asia (cf. the first part of this report). Had Augustus been less wary of publicity, I am sure the park would have been one of the more famous productions of the Gilded Age.

Whch Josiah was eight or nine years old, he asked Elias how long Miss Adams had lived at the estate.

"All her life," Elias said. Josiah, Elias, and Drusilla were following a deer path near the eastern entrance of the park, and Elias's lesson to his children that day concerned the practical genius of the deer. (When building or repairing paths for humans to take through the park, step one was to look for where the deer had already cleared the way. The path will never be straight, but it will be smart, and that's what matters: each turn has a purpose, whether to steer clear of old fallen trees or to cross a brook at the easiest point.)

The children were distracted, inattentive. Their mother was only a few months dead, and the land's consolations felt few. In the sleepless nights after Charlotte's death, Elias had barely restrained himself from screaming at the indifferent sky, tearing grass from the meadows until his hands bled raw, striking a match to burn the forests barren. Charlotte's cancer was not the fault of the land, it had nothing to do with the land, yet in his grief Elias wanted some sign that this place knew the ache that tore his veins with each heartbeat. His life had been devoted to the land's own pain, and, in his selfish and human way, he wanted some acknowledgment of his devotion. Soon enough, as he walked the deer paths or sat at the edge of the lake or climbed to the rocky top of Gray Mountain to see above it all, the land gave him something more than acknowledgment — it welcomed him back to the rhythms of the swaying branches, the lilt of the water against the shore, the cadence of birds in flight, the wonder of squirrels and chipmunks bounding in double time, the resonant patterns of insects humming over surfaces and scurrying into the soil. Within those rhythms and patterns, he felt Charlotte brushing a breeze against his cheek. She had been welcomed through their marriage, bound to this place, and at death returned. (As always, the body of any Thornton was returned to the family rather than given to a funeral home, and Elias, Valeria, the children, and Charlotte's mother had buried her in the place near the farmhouse where generations of Thorntons had gone to rest, and only a dozen miles or so from the town cemetery where others of Charlotte's family, including her father, had preceded her.) He knew she was here, knew she was not gone but changed, dispersed through the soil and water and air; but the knowledge did not hold the comfort of hands, of smiles, of kisses, tears, laughter, and all the small joys of ordinary presence.

"Miss Adams has lived a very long life," Josiah said.

"The land keeps her alive," Drusilla said.

"I know that," Josiah said. Ever since their mother's death, Josiah had bristled when his older sister offered knowledge. "What I don't know is *why*."

"Soon," Elias said, "I will take you both up to the mansion to see some of the history that lives there. You will understand better then. For now, though, don't feel jealous of the long life Miss Adams lives. Think of her like one of the fossils we found. A piece of something captured outside of time. All our ancestors are at peace here as part of the land. That includes your mother. She is here with us. The trees, the grass, the water, all of it is part of us, and we are from it and will be part of it again. That is the way. For Miss Adams, it is … different. She has been exiled. She lives outside time. That is all you need to know right now."

It was more than his parents had told him when he was his children's age, and Elias felt the heavy inadequacy of the words, but he hoped Drusilla and Josiah, so sensitive and quick to understand most things, would find some comfort in the blessings of their own lives and not waste themselves in jealousy of what they would soon enough know to be a curse.

Excerpts from the report by Dr. Steven A. Baird to the Hoadley Foundation, September 2017, cont'd:

Once, attending a conference at Dartmouth College, I drove the hour north to Colton and its neighbors. I found the park's gate and talked to a few local people out for a walk, but if any of them knew anything about the place, they were not willing to talk to a stranger about it. The nearest public library was open, and I spent some time with what passed for archives there, but there was nothing I had not already seen.[3]

Then, as I began to feel that I had visited enough small-town libraries to last a lifetime and read more than any human being ought to read of local newspapers from the 1930s — and that, more than anything, I was wasting this Foundation's generous grant — I received a letter from Valeria Adams in Colton, New

---

3. Thanks to the generosity of the Hoadley Foundation, I have been able to search numerous other small-town libraries and historical society archives — though, as the first part of this report shows, with no enlightening discovery. My conclusion here, however, will point to extraordinary new opportunities ahead.

Hampshire dated September 1, 2017.

The letter was written in blue ink, with the telltale fluidity of a fountain pen, on gilded stationery in a sure and elegant script:

> Dear Dr. Baird:
> I write to invite you to visit me at my family estate. You are aware of the location. There is much I hope to be able to share with you about our family's fortunes and misfortunes. If you were to arrive within the next two weeks, I would be grateful. Drive to the Colton gate and my assistant, Mr. Josiah Thornton, will lead you to the house.
> Sincerely,
> Valeria Adams

Though my inclination was to go immediately to Adams Park, I did not want to seem as excited as I was, so I waited a few days (some of the longest days of my life) and took the first morning bus out of Boston to Hanover, New Hampshire, where I rented a car and drove to Colton, arriving in the late afternoon. Just as I stopped at the gate, it opened. A man of about my age, wearing cargo pants and the sort of many-pocketed vest I associate with hunters, stood in front of a dark green Land Rover and beckoned me forward. I pulled up beside him and lowered the window. He introduced himself as Josiah Thornton.

The Land Rover led me over a well-tended dirt road through a forest that soon opened to fields and meadows, with a pond (or maybe lake) in the distance and rolling hills beyond it. The road curved away from the water and up what I soon saw was the side of a craggy hill or small mountain. At the top stood something more than a house — *castle* would not be an inappropriate word, though it rambled more than I think of castles doing, as if once upon a time it was a modest, symmetrical structure, but with the passage of decades it sprouted, branched, and spread more by blind will than by design. Massive timber beams framed a stone building of at least three storeys, a structure redolent of both French Renaissance and Gothic Revival styles, though what I would come to know as its eastern wing, dominated as it was by a massive conical tower in the middle of the structure, is architecturally unique in my experience.[4] Around the driveway sat modest grounds dominated by stone and lichen. Most impressive was the view out beyond the few small trees around the house, a view of wilderness, not a building in sight.

Josiah Thornton saw me staring out at the horizon. He said that even though he had lived his life on the grounds, the view here never failed to fill him with awe. He said that Augustus Adams had begged, borrowed, and sometimes flat-out stolen all he would need to make sure that in any direction he looked from the house, he would only see land he controlled. I was, of

---

4. The closest analogue to the tower that I know of is that of the original Moyamensing Prison in Philadelphia, designed by Thomas Ustick Walter (1804-1887), though in the images I have seen, that tower was much smaller and less dominant than the one at the center of the east wing of the Adams mansion. Moyamensing is perhaps most famous for being the place of imprisonment and execution in 1896 of serial killer H.H. Holmes (born 1861 as Herman Webster Mudgett in Gilmanton, New Hampshire). See *H. H. Holmes: The True History of the White City Devil* by Adam Seltzer (New York: Skyhorse Publishing, 2017).

course, amazed because from where we stood, the view seemed to be vast, perhaps a quarter of the whole state. Josiah Thornton said it was something of an illusion. The hill feels more elevated than it really is, he said, and the land is carefully managed so as to maintain quite a few different habitats, which has the nice effect of making the vista seem to be miles and miles and miles when, in truth, the entire park is only about twenty-five thousand acres. ("Only" is the word he used.)

Josiah then led me up a cascade of steps and into the central area of the house, where we stood in a foyer clearly designed to make visitors think they had entered a cathedral. Immense stone stairways rose left and right; the entire floor was an intricate mosaic of blue, white, red, and green; huge windows sat beneath an arched stone ceiling far above; pillars held immense candelabras and what were, I am sure, priceless sculptures from ancient civilizations.

I followed Josiah past the stairs and down a hallway at the far back of the foyer. After making our way through a maze of doors, we came to a relatively modest room dominated by a series of many-paned windows with an unimpeded view of the park. The furniture was antique — it seemed to me to be of the Arts and Crafts aesthetic, a product of great skill and vision but determinedly functional.

Josiah offered me food and drink, but too overwhelmed by the vista and the situation to make any sort of choice, I only requested water. I stood entranced at the windows while he went off to some inner room — I imagined him filling a crystal pitcher from a giant fountain sculpture of Pan (fed by a mountain spring!), but I expect it was a kitchen.

Within moments, I heard a voice behind me say my name.

———————

After Valeria told him she was preparing to leave the estate, Elias found himself wandering through the woods, then out across fields of tall grass and around the western shore of the large pond Valeria's grandfather had named Lake Vico. Without consciously deciding on a destination, Elias crosses through a grove of trees and down to the sunken lands. He has not been to the old hunting cabin in many years, but there it stands in front of him, its porch rotting away, its clapboards long ago scrubbed of color, its roofline sagging. Though he was born two decades after any person had (to his knowledge, at least) set foot in the cabin, Elias feels an amused kinship with the structure as he, too, sags under the weight of years, his skin scarred and hardened by weather, his body accommodating its own fair share of rot. The cabin dates to 1895, one of the later structures built for the visitors who came to the preserve, but it was not visitors who found their fate in it.

Elias wonders when Valeria last wandered out here. Likely not in many decades, perhaps not since the day when everything changed for her family, the day her real life began. Nearly a hundred years ago. His parents told Elias everything, of course, helped him see that what Valeria perceived to be a truth was ferociously incomplete. They also helped him understand why that incomplete understanding needed to remain undisturbed, uncomplicated. It was not until Valeria herself told Elias the story (during his first year taking over the maintenance of the preserve from his father — long ago now), that he learned how she understood their families' shared histories.

"You know about my illness when I was young," Valeria said all those years ago as they sat together in the smaller dining room of the mansion on the mountain; their dinner that October night, Elias remembers, a simple pie made with elk meat. "Your father was little more than a toddler, but he was there in the farmhouse when your grandparents heard me tell them of the terrible pain and suffering I felt while I was at boarding school in New York and then when I left home again to enter society."

"They asked you if you had been to the cave beneath the mountain," Elias said, eager to show how well his parents had prepared him, how knowledgeable he was, how unafraid.

"Yes. I was shocked that they knew about it. I had thought it was a secret, and I cherished all secrets. But your people have always known about it. The cave. The mountain. *This* mountain," she said wistfully, as if only now realizing where they sat. "They knew immediately what had happened. The consequences of my explorations. They knew everything. Not because they had spied on me. They had not. But they knew about this place, about the land, its history, our history together. Their sympathy was a great gift to me. Your grandmother said it was no wonder that I should wander. Perfectly natural for a curious girl bereft of friends to explore the land where she had spent her life. They did not make me feel ashamed for my transgression nor for my illness when I was away. They were kind people. Gentle.

"Your grandparents helped my own family understand. A chronic condition, a cross I would have to bear. Something like that. Nobody told me what they said. All I know is that I did not have to leave here after that, not for very long, at least. Enough to be out in the world now and then to get my name into the society columns. A week here, a week there. It was enough, though, for me to encounter a lovely girl, Lily Davenport, a true beauty, daughter of a shipping magnate. We fell in love. Furiously in love. It was not something we could talk about, of course. But, as I said, I enjoyed having secrets. Lily was my best secret."

At that moment, in Elias's memory at least, Valeria's face shone with new light, as if a ray of moonlight came through a window near the ceiling, but there were no windows of any sort in the dining room. The light passed quickly.

"Things were not well in my family at that time if they had ever been. My mother was living on gin and cigarettes. My father was trying to keep the family businesses going while also trying to fend off the forces unleashed here. My brother was making a fool of himself at the local tavern night after night while also now and then torturing expensive animals on the land.

"And then he, my brother Claude, found out about Lily. He saw us. It was at the hunting cabin out in the sunken lands. Hardly anyone ever used it, and there were few visitors to the park anymore, so Lily and I would have our assignations there. It seemed safe. It *was* safe. Except that my brother enjoyed stalking me. He always had. I thought I had learned to outwit him, but love makes us all careless. Flagrantly careless. And so, he traced us to the cabin. Probably quite easily. Once he found us, he watched, I'm sure, for quite a while. He was always a voyeur. It was one of his greatest passions: watching, savoring. He waited until Lily and I were fully engaged with each other, and then he flung open the door like an actor in a melodrama. Rather proud of himself, I suppose. He attacked Lily terribly. Not sexually. He was not a sexual man. Just force, physical force. He all but threw her across the room."

After a pause, Valeria said, "You must have, at the very least, a vague idea of what happened next. Your family—"

"My father," Elias had said quickly (nervous and uncertain, not yet accustomed to conversation with Valeria), "told me your brother was punished, the whole family punished, and that was when you inherited the estate."

Valeria smiled slightly, but Elias did not know if she was amused or perplexed or simply patronizing him. "That is all he said?"

Elias nodded, afraid to speak lest his words give away his lie, even if that lie were something like a truth. His father had said much about the family and Valeria and the estate but only briefly mentioned Claudius Adams. That he had said more about the inheritance was not something Valeria needed to know.

"Living through it, even as a child, does not, I suppose, make it something one wants to relate in detail. Nonetheless. You need to know the truth. You cannot do your job in ignorance."

She refilled her glass with wine from a decanter on the table. Elias had hardly touched his own glass. "This is a fine Bordeaux," she said. "I know nothing about it except that it is expensive and that the manager of the wine importer of which I own a controlling share told me it is among the best bottles he has ever held. Not to your taste?"

Elias lifted his glass. "It is excellent," he said. "I am simply a little out of sorts."

"No shame in that," Valeria said. "A mark in your favor, in fact. A testament to your sensitivity. The elk we ate tonight, did you kill it yourself?"

"Yes," Elias said. "My father and I. I shot it. We stripped it together."

"Do you enjoy hunting?"

"No," Elias said. "But it must be done. We must eat. And the land is limited. The larger animals, especially, will suffer if we let their numbers reach too many. They will starve. There are no other predators here, really, and so it falls to us. The role of the predator."

"Long ago, my grandfather, Augustus, brought wolves in. Unlike my father or my brother, Augustus was truly interested in what now we might call ecology. He hoped when he bought the land that he could create a self-sustaining preserve. It almost worked."

"What happened to the wolves?"

"They got expensive. Unlike the guests, who always feared to violate any of the rules and thus only hunted what they were allowed to hunt, the wolves imagined themselves to be free. I don't know the details. Augustus kept records of everything, and you are welcome to look through the papers if you want. For whatever reason, the wolves only lasted a short time."

Elias sipped his wine. Valeria pushed her plate a few inches away from herself.

"As I said, you must know what happened in 1931 if you are to do your job effectively. So I will tell you."

She stared at her plate. She closed her eyes, breathed deeply.

She opened her eyes and said, in a clear and even voice: "After my brother did what he did to Lily, he brushed himself off, smiled at me, and walked out of the cabin. And then he was torn limb from limb, very slowly, as he walked through the woods. I had learned from what I found in the cave how to resonate with the land. That is how I think of it. As resonance, a kind of rhythm. The land felt my heartbeat, and I felt … something beyond language. I made a request, or perhaps a wish, and the land replied. Ancient roots reached out from deep in the ground and found his flesh. The soil scraped his skin raw. It was a sight to behold, the ground itself rising up, shredding his clothes, lacerating his skin, the roots and vines flaying him, his screams muffled by the tree branch that punched its way into his mouth and down his throat, pulverizing all that was inside him, returning him to the land he did not deserve to walk upon."

She had not looked at Elias while she told her story; now she stared at him with unblinking eyes, her gaze intense and yet unemotional, inquisitive, seeking any response. But Elias sat still, unmoving, unable to move.

"And then the others," Valeria said. "Each in their own way. I lured them outside to be taken by the land they thought they owned, controlled, dominated." She sat back in her chair and smiled. "It was a long time ago. Nonetheless, I still remember the sense of awakening to my own self, my destiny, my — oh, it all sounds so grandiose. But it *is* grandiose. Now and then, if we are lucky, we get to experience something that feels both like liberation and like fate. Now and then, we wield power."

She sighed. "It does not last, though. Fate has its way with liberation. And though they say power corrupts, I rather think it corrodes." She ran her finger over the rim of her wine glass. "No need for my philosophizing. You are young and have much ahead of you. Now, the night grows long, and you need the facts, not an old lady's musings." She dutifully drank the last of her glass of wine. "Lily and I lived here happily together until 1956, when she left this place. Do you remember her at all from your childhood?"

"A bit," Elias said, not entirely truthfully. As a child, he had been frightened of Valeria and stayed as far away from the mansion as possible. He had a vague memory of a tall blonde woman he had thought might be Valeria's older sister. But the memory fell away in his mind like summer rain.

"By the end, she had grown despondent, lonely," Valeria said. "We loved each other through it all, but she did not have the long family connection here, and she persisted in thinking the outside world might be a place of kindness and compassion and joy. She learned otherwise. She withered away, dead within a year."

Elias remembers Valeria turning aside then, her face hidden in darkness. He imagined she was wiping a tear from her eye, but now he doubts she was so sentimental. In all the years since, she has never uttered a sentimental word, and with the exception of one other moment, she barely revealed any emotion at all, as if she were made of the same rock as the mountain. Still, he likes to remember her that night in his own way, likes to imagine that a human chord in Valeria sounded then and still resonates, that a pang of regret or longing released a tear she resisted for decades, a tear for the only love she ever allowed herself.

He has never entered the hunting cabin where Claudius Adams tracked, then trapped, Valeria and Lily. It is not that

Elias holds any superstitions about the place, for it is no more (or less) enchanted than any other spot in Adams Park, but he thinks the building and its history ought to be allowed some privacy, that the memories it contains are best left to rot away with the roof and walls and floors.

For as long as anyone can remember, the area near the cabin has been called the sunken lands, a low flat place that often floods in the spring when the snows melt, though the cabin sits high enough on the slope of a gentle hill to avoid the water. Elias has never wondered what gave the location its shape or its name, but he would not be surprised to learn it was a graveyard once, perhaps even a mass grave dug after one of the terrible events Augustus Adams arranged for his wealthy guests to enjoy. He knows it was here that the land reclaimed Claudius Adams, but he does not know where Valeria and Claudius's father, Tiberius, fell, nor what became of any of the other family members. (The family members other than Augustus; the fate of the old man is the one he knows best and most intimately.) Valeria never provided details and dislikes talking about the days of her inheritance in 1931.

It was all so long ago. And yet the past lives in the present here, lives not like memory but like the light of stars — the stars themselves long dead, the light held alive in the distance of the sky.

"Enough dithering," Elias says to himself, his soft voice swallowed by the sunken lands.

Late afternoon sun draws long shadows from the cabin as he turns to make his way back up the hill, across the field, and through the woods to the path connecting his family's farmhouse with the mansion on the mountain. He needs to share with his family what Valeria told him today of her intentions. There is much to prepare for, much they have spent generations planning for, much he hoped he would not live to see.

Excerpts from the report by Dr. Steven A. Baird to the Hoadley Foundation, September 2017, cont'd:

After receiving the invitation from Valeria Adams, I imagined her to be an elderly woman. Tiberius Adams had a daughter, Valeria, who was born in 1903, but she would undoubtedly be long dead, and I wondered how the Adams name had continued, whether there had been, perhaps, a birth of a boy out of wedlock, which, for all the scandal it would have created during that era, would at least have assured the name lived on. On the other hand, *Adams* is one of the more common names in the United States, and it would certainly be possible for an Adams of one line to marry an Adams of another. The elegant stationary, handwriting, and ink of the invitation had suggested someone with a sense of propriety quite lost in our informal age, so my imagination produced a Valeria Adams deep into her later years.

I turned from the window to see a woman likely not much older than myself, just barely approaching middle age. Her skin was as pale as the modest white dress she wore, and long brown hair hung straight down to her waist. Her face was sharp, angular, but her eyes were warm.

She welcomed me, we exchanged pleasantries and insisted on first names, and Josiah brought a large silver tray with glasses and a porcelain pitcher filled with ice water. Valeria Adams then told me that she was the daughter of Tiberius Franklin Adams, and that her late brother, Claudius (known as Claude), was in fact my great-grandfather on my mother's side. I will confess that at first I thought I misheard her, and said so. When she repeated this information, I laughed. She smiled gently, then related a most extraordinary story.

That story is not relevant to this report because I believe that in all its details it is fiction. It is a tale of mysterious forces and people who do not age. Quite ridiculous. Clearly, something went terribly awry with Valeria Adams and her family, whoever they may be, and their insanity (forgive me for labeling it such, but I can think of no other word) has been buttressed and protected by their great wealth.

Or perhaps — and, indeed, this is most likely — she was simply having fun with an obsessive scholar who has poked his nose too often into her business.

Nonetheless, I believe Valeria Adams (if that is, indeed, her name), while fabricating a delusional tale of her own family, was speaking something like the truth about *my* family. I know of nothing that contradicts anything she told me about my ancestors, and, in fact, the tale she told explains why, for instance, my mother would have kept an old postcard of Adams Park and Colton, New Hampshire. The information Valeria Adams shared has, for the first time in my life, sparked an interest in me in genealogy, and I expect some of my future work, whether for scholarly purposes or simply for my own edification, will be an investigation into my heritage.

First, though, I will see Valeria Adams again. She has asked me to return to Adams Park, as she would like to show me the archives there. I look forward to writing a second report of my activities, activities made possible by the generous support of this Foundation.

———————

Steven Baird's is a familiar name, a name Elias first heard after he had been overseeing the preserve for a decade or so. Elias's father had been dead for a year, Drusilla and Josiah were children but both old enough to help out a bit, and in the months after his father's death he had met with Valeria Adams even less than usual, which was not a problem, as the park was healthy and mostly took care of itself, but he missed their chats. He wondered if, perhaps, finally, her age had begun to affect her. When he did see her, she was brusque; not unfriendly, but obviously preoccupied with matters other than the land. Nondescript but expensive cars climbed the mountain at all hours. Clearly, Valeria had summoned various agents of the fortune, people who had been rare visitors before but for a few months suddenly came and went from the mansion with regularity. Elias was grateful that they never ventured anywhere else on the property; he did not have the staff to handle such an incursion.

Usually, when Valeria needed something from Elias, she

summoned him with a few bleeps of the emergency signal on the radio, but that day when Steven Baird's name suddenly became an important one in all their lives, Valeria called him on the radio directly. "Elias? Elias, are you out there?" he heard from the jeep as he shoveled gravel onto a road that had washed out in a recent rainstorm.

He picked up the radio and answered.

"Elias, I wonder if you might have dinner with me this evening. I would like to discuss some developments."

He said he would be happy to join her, then asked if he ought to bring anything, though of course he knew the answer because the answer was always the same (the kitchen staff would take care of everything). Still, it was polite to ask.

"You need bring nothing," Valeria said. "Please be here by six."

Unlike the other times Elias had dined with Valeria, that night she could hardly sit still, she had no interest in small talk, and touched little of her food, though the staff had laid out a feast that could have filled the stomachs of a few dozen people.

"I must tell you," Valeria said, "the most exciting news. We have found an Adams ancestor who, I expect, can be cultivated to return here to the estate, and will in all likelihood, eventually, be quite happy to do so. Isn't that marvelous?"

Elias nodded, his mouth full. He had been working all day and had hardly paid attention to hunger. The pheasant and wild boar on the table were especially well cooked, and he filled his plate with them, then felt like a barbarian as he grabbed one mouthful after another. He added bread, carrots, broccoli, rice to his plate and tried to eat them less ravenously.

Valeria could not stay in her seat. She paced the dining

room as if impatient for Elias to finish.

"You are still young, relatively speaking, and I know you can't really appreciate what it means for me to see the possibility of change, of freedom, even if — well, of course, none of us know what it may mean, this is uncharted territory, but nonetheless, it is — don't you think? — terribly exciting. Terribly, terribly exciting."

"Do you mean it will give you the freedom to leave here?" Elias asked. He tried not to sound accusatory or anything other than neutral, but Valeria's smile sank.

"Are you not happy for me?"

"Yes," he said. "I'm just trying to make sure I understand. So I can plan."

"Of course. And I will share it all with you. It will take quite some time, do not worry yourself right now, all I want is for you to be happy for me." She returned to her seat and pushed some carrots and mashed potato around on her plate. "I am sorry I am so out of sorts. I had all but given up hope. Surely you understand. You, better than anyone, no?" Across the long table, Elias forced what he hoped was a compassionate smile. "For decades," Valeria said, "I have assumed that my days would continue in this drip, drip, drip of endless sameness, the queen of the land, bound in its nourishing and stifling embrace — but then some years ago I learned that a suitable ancestor was out there, a child, and he could be cultivated, he could be perfect — and we watched him grow, we did all that we could to nurture him without showing our hand, without spoiling this one perfect opportunity, and now it seems, yes — yes, it has all been worth it."

"I am very happy for you," Elias said.

"His name is Steven. Steven Baird. He is a brilliant student fascinated by history. Quite solitary. He has discovered a love of archival work."

"And he is an ancestor?"

"Yes! Astonishing, isn't it? The great-grandson of my brother Claudius and a servant girl who worked here. Claude repeatedly and brutally raped her, not out of any sort of lust, which I don't think he ever felt for an actual human being, because he cared nothing for people, but rather he saw her, and everyone, as a way to exert power, dominance."

"And she escaped?" Elias said. He had never heard a story of anyone escaping the Adams men.

"Yes. She was a quiet girl whose parents had come to this country recently but who were both murdered by a mob in Boston that went out one weekend night in search of dark-skinned people with foreign accents, people to harass and, it turned out, to kill. She was working somewhere across the city and came home to corpses. We called her Sara, though her name was Safiyya. She fled us when she became pregnant. She changed her name to Aisha Smith, then soon enough she changed it again to Anna, then got married, and so mostly appears in genealogical records and such as Anna Henderson, a bland enough name to disappear with in this country. But I kept track. I hoped that after Claude's death she might return. It would have been nice to see her again. Of course, she did not return, and I do not blame her. This was a place of horror in her life. I understood. But one of the things I learned from my father, and from your ancestors as well, is that we must never lose track of our family, our blood. And so we paid attention. After Lily left, I began to think about what might allow me to leave. Truly leave. Eventually, I understood. And so, we are here, now. An ancestor has been found. We will do everything we must do to cultivate and to protect Steven Baird. Sometime in the next ten or twenty years, maybe longer, but soon enough — sometime, he will come here. And I, finally, will be able to go."

She sat back in her chair, seemingly exhausted by her frantic talking.

"If only your father had lived a few months longer. If only he had known. He always hoped I might go free."

Tears glistened on her cheeks. She held her hand to her face and wept.

Quietly, Elias stood and walked out of the mansion, down the mountain, and back to the farmhouse. There was much to prepare. Elias wished his father were still alive to consult with. His father had always enjoyed and appreciated the Thornton family legacy more than Elias, and, as Valeria sensed, had even looked forward to the day when the prophecies they had passed down generation after generation would come true. He doubted whether his father had cared any more than he himself did about Valeria's freedom. Her leaving or staying was inconsequential. The return of an Adams ancestor, though — that was cause for celebration, a day long anticipated.

The Thorntons hid much from every Adams who had ever been here. That was their duty and purpose. The prophecy was the greatest responsibility, and Elias felt the great weight of that responsibility when he inherited it. It promised much.

He has always looked forward to the glory to come, but the night he first heard Steven Baird's name, he, too, wanted to weep for the future day when he and his children would have to carry out the task set for them so long ago.

The diary of Dr. Steven S. Baird is a 5"x 8.25" bound, hardback notebook with a black cover and ruled pages. Its binding is weakened and a substantial number of pages in the middle have been torn out and are missing. The first entries in the diary consist of three loose pages printed from a computer file, folded in quarters and placed at the beginning of the notebook. In the notebook itself, most of the entries are written by the same hand in blue ink, though some entries are in black ink. For the sake of this transcription, dates have been standardized to day, month, year format, which is how they begin, though later dates are more irregular in style. Ellipses in brackets indicate excisions by the editors of repetitive or irrelevant material.

The diary was received by Dimond Library at the University of New Hampshire on or about August 25, 2018, and then delivered to the Milne Special Collections and Archives. A letter accompanying the diaries indicated that it was a donation to the "Adams Park Collection", but no such collection exists, nor is there record of such a collection at the University of New Hampshire or any other institution. Dr. Baird did not respond to inquiries. The diary remains in storage.

7 June 2016

The manuscript of *Sleepy Hollows: Intersections of Nature and Culture in Westchester County 1683-1895* was accepted by SUNY Press a few months ago after positive peer review. I have been working on minor revisions requested. Nearly finished with all that, and damned tired of the whole project — which began with all the work for the dissertation (5 or 6 years of research and writing) then revision into a book (2 years, off and on), then the interminable process of submission to presses and waiting for responses, then revising to my editor's suggestions, then re-submission, then waiting for responses to peer review, now revising final little things to show the reviewers that I paid some attention to their comments. By the time it is published, it will have been a decade, more or less, from beginning to end. It is a wonder any academic books get published at all!

For the last month or so, I have felt a stirring of interest in a new project. At first, it was not an interest in any one project itself, but rather a desire to return to the archives. (Which archives? Any!) The urge grew in me as I taught classes at Boston University and Lesley, feeling ever more bounced around and adjunctified, barely able to pay my rent despite working what felt like 32-hour days, 10 days a week. Now and then I allow myself to fantasize that with a book out I will be able to land a job on the tenure track somewhere, a job with a respectable salary and benefits, but I try not to indulge that fantasy too often, as I know the chances are slim. I honestly don't know what else I will do with myself, though, and if I think about the likely possibilities, despair becomes overwhelming. Better to outline new projects and continue on like a fool.

It seems to me that I ought to try to turn my interest in Adams Park into something. At the least, I ought to be able to get a journal article out of it. I have a box of photocopies, printouts, books, and random ephemera in the back of the closet, a box I have hauled from Brooklyn to Texas to Fargo to Boston over the last 13 years and which I ought at the very least to index and begin seeking strands and possibilities within. I don't even understand the obsession. It is like a quiet hum in my brain, a nagging sense wherever I am that I ought to at least keep my eyes out for something to do with Adams Park, Augustus Adams, or Colton, New Hampshire. And I have done so, never finding any great amount of information, but often finding bits and pieces which feel like they are beginning to add up to something. Add up to what, I don't know, but figuring it out would make a good new project. [...]

23 June 2016

Working through the box of Adams Park materials has been a great pleasure. It has felt like a reunion with old friends. But it's not all old friends, at least in the sense of being familiar — some things I had either completely forgotten or never bothered to look at before I stashed them away. Thankfully, it all feels more coherent than I remembered.

For the sake of refreshing my memory, a few important dates:

1765: Alasdair Adams born in Scotland to a family of merchants whose ventures often ended in failure

1783: Alasdair Adams emigrates to United States, establishes himself in the timber industry (big gap in documentation around this)

1785: Alasdair Adams marries Eleanor Warren, whose

family arrived on the American continent not long after the landing of the *Mayflower* and boasted prominent branches throughout the United States and England. Eleanor's own father was a modest lawyer who seems never to have spent much time with his somewhat more successful siblings and significantly more successful cousins, perhaps because he tended his sickly wife, who lived only a few years after Eleanor's birth.

1786: Birth of Robert Adams, Sr.

(Between 1785 and 1825, the family business expanded beyond timber to shipping and eventually finance. Records I have found are murky, as if Alasdair and, later, Robert Adams deliberately sought to keep their involvement in businesses unclear. This pattern continues really until Tiberius's brief venture from c. 1896-1903 in making Adams Park a tourist attraction.)

1809: Robert Adams marries Catherine Benoit

1812: Birth of Robert Adams, Jr. (after Frances [1810] and Marie [1811]; Marie died 3 days after birth)

1824: Robert Adams, Jr. marries Eleanor Tucker

1825: Birth of **Alexander Adams**, death of Eleanor Tucker in childbirth

1847: Alasdair Adams dies at age 81 of unknown cause.

Alexander Adams marries Dorothy Franklin (April), who gives birth to **Geoffrey Adams** (October), who will rename himself **Augustus**.

1857: Death of Robert Adams, Sr. at age 70, cause unknown.

(Sometime around 1858-1860, Alexander Adams expanded the family business to railroads and other forms of transportation. He worked diligently to hide this, but the business — or, rather, businesses — had become so sprawling that it was impossible for the family's extraordinary power not to be noticed. There is definite evidence of holdings throughout Latin America and possibly in Africa, but I have not had a chance to work with archives that might provide any detail.)

1864: Death of Robert Adams, Jr. at age 52 in March of pneumonia. Death of Alexander Adams at age 39 of tuberculosis in November. (Something made me note that this cause seems suspicious, but I can't remember why.) Geoffrey, 17 years old, inherits the business and within a year renames himself Augustus.

1866: Augustus Adams purchases first plot of land in Colton, NH.

1870: Augustus Adams marries Ruth Gibson of Oxford, MS.

1872: Mention in the *Providence Journal* that "presently,

it is said that there is no type of good entering or leaving New England that does not pass through a business run by Augustus Adams, often many businesses. His family's prominence in the business sphere goes back generations, but the present success is very much of his own creation." If anything, this understates the situation, since Alexander owned controlling interests in businesses throughout the United States and Canada: he was significantly involved with railroads, banks, countless small retail stores from Maine to Chicago, warehouses, factories, mines... Yet unlike other wealthy and powerful men of his era, Augustus did not put his name on things. Indeed, he went to considerable effort to create a series of trusts-within-trusts to obscure just how much wealth and power he had. I doubt there is any way to know now all that he controlled.

1873: After some miscarriages and possibly a stillbirth (records unclear), Ruth Adams gives birth to **Tiberius Franklin Adams**.

1895: Death of Augustus Adams at age 47 of heart failure.

1896: Tiberius opens Adams Park to the public for a few days in August and October. This is the only time it is actually named as "Adams Park".

1903: The final year Adams Park is opened for a few days to the public, as best I can determine. (No advertisements, postcards, etc. seem to be from any later years.) Massive fires throughout the state destroy 200,000 acres of New

Hampshire land, with 84,000 acres of northern forest destroyed. The fires reach Adams Park on the north, west, and eastern sides, but apparently cause no notable damage within the borders. (Fire caused by exceptionally dry summer conditions and, in the north country, rampant logging plus sparks from trains hauling timber.) Significant rain soon follows the fires, causing landslides across many clearcut areas, including areas on the northern edge of Adams Park. An unpublished memoir in the New York Public Library by Elliot Davenport, who owned various transport companies and seems to have been a friend of Tiberius Adams, suggests that at least one person was killed in the fires and/or the landslides, but I have not found any confirmation of this.

1905: Tiberius Adams marries Miriam Chappell (February), who gives birth to Valeria Adams (December 7).

1908: Miriam Adams gives birth to Claudius Adams.

1931: Last record of any Adams other than Valeria on legal documents. No further notice in newspapers of anything related to Adams Park.

I am reminded of something I noticed early in my research: there are only two times where there is anything like robust historical material concerning the Adams sons and brothers (and I am also reminded that *all* of the historical material concerns Adams sons and brothers, not wives and daughters) — first, on either side of the Civil War, with the success of Alexander in expanding the business far beyond the timber company founded in the late 18th century, and then Augustus continuing that expansion; and, secondly, the few years at the fin de siècle where Tiberius Adams seems to have yearned for public recognition. Alexander and, especially, Augustus were true robber barons, men who bought, sold, and consolidated businesses like little toys. About Tiberius, though, I know very little.

The name *Adams* makes searching far more difficult than it would be for a family with even a slightly less common surname. However, the strain of Adams that produced Alexander, Augustus, Tiberius, etc. came from a pretty narrow family tree. Not incestuous, at least as far as I can tell, just not very fertile. While tracing every Adams family in the U.S. would be a herculean endeavor, tracing this particular set of Adamses is less of a challenge. Or, rather, the challenges of tracing this family are not caused by how common their surname is or how plentiful their relations.

[...] While I dream of stumbling upon a lost memoir (or even just a thorough puff piece for a newspaper), it would not change the fascinating — perplexing — fact that from Augustus Adams onward, the family mostly kept out of the public eye and escaped the embalmments of history we would expect for anyone of their class and power. Aside from Adams Park, there are no monuments with their names on them. No buildings, no statues — not even, as far as I've been able to determine, a commemorative plaque anywhere.

Unsurprisingly, then, there is no meaningful scholarship on

this Adams family or Adams Park. If other scholars have attempted studying them, I am unaware of it; even if they did, they would not get far. After all these years of searching, I know little more than what I have written here.

———————

In his first years as manager of the preserve, Elias would often bring game or vegetables up to the mountain during the day, and sometimes Valeria would see him and they would talk about the weather or the changing seasons or the endless challenge of keeping the wild pigs from finding a way through the fence and out into the nearby towns, where the pigs inevitably ended up rooting through people's gardens, causing uproar. At first, Valeria's conversations were superficial and business-like, but she warmed to Elias quickly, and even told him he was by far the most intelligent and sensitive of the Thornton men she had known.

Now and then they wander to the space everyone has always called "the observatory": a long, narrow room that stretches across the western side of the mansion's first floor, with vast windows overlooking the preserve. The walls are painted a flat beige and adorned only with brass sconces for lighting. The furniture is beautifully crafted but simple, and though he does not know its origin, Elias suspects it was bought by Valeria herself, since it lacks the ostentation common to the many rooms furnished with the choices of other members of the family, whose tastes led them toward more imperial decoration.

The moment in the observatory that holds most vividly in Elias's memory was an afternoon after a great summer storm blustered havoc throughout the park. Elias had come up to the mountain to give Valeria a report of the storm's effects, but Valeria had seemed distracted, uninterested. They stood together at the windows and stared out in silence for some time. Meadows spread out beneath the mountain, then forests grew thick across rolling hills that reached to Lake Vico's shores. The sky, so recently a cacophony of slate and granite, now burned blue.

A flock of turkeys scampered through a meadow toward the trees.

After long silence, Valeria said, "A peaceful, beautiful scene. It sings to the part of our soul that traces all the way back to the earliest ancestors." Elias thinks now there was sarcasm, even bitterness, in her tone, but trying to divine Valeria's thoughts via her voice is not a skill he ever honed, and all those years ago, naivety still charted his way.

"A landscape for painters and poets," Elias said. "You would hardly believe that just a few hours ago the whole planet seemed to be rising up against it all."

"Never trust the peace of this place," Valeria said. "Never trust the beauty."

"The beauty," Elias said, "is hard to ignore. Even though I have lived most of the days of my life here. Still, even now, the beauty is—"

"Undeniable. The sublime expanse. The natural wonder. The glory of nature." Valeria pressed her hand against a windowpane. "And yet, what you see there — all of it, every acre and every inch — is a cemetery. A burial ground."

Elias does not remember saying anything in response, but his face must have betrayed his confusion at words that he had never expected her to utter. Could she guess the extent of the truth she spoke?

"I have been organizing my grandfather's papers," Valeria said. "I feel that I ought to know him better, that everything we are doing will be more successful if we can perceive his point of view. To that end, I have been reading the records. He kept extensive, precise records."

"What have you discovered?"

"More than I wish to say. And too much to keep to myself."

Valeria gestured for Elias to sit. A crystal pitcher of lemonade had appeared with two glasses on a side table. Valeria poured them both a drink.

"What the records show is that along with the hundreds of animals he brought here, Augustus imported *people* — starting with twenty-seven slaves he bought from traders in Mississippi before the end of the Civil War and transported here to begin the work of transforming the land. Their first task was to build the miles of fence that would imprison them. Not one of those people ever stepped outside the perimeter again. Two were lost to illness, but the others became, after the war, playthings for bitter — or perhaps just nostalgic — plantation owners, men who paid very good money to come up here for a week of ... fun. These men were freely allowed to whip and rape and even, if they paid well enough, to murder. As the last of the slaves were being killed, Augustus brought in entire train cars of Cheyenne people, giving them time to establish little areas of their own in the park, then allowing his friends — his colleagues, his peers — to hunt them. These obscenely rich men loved pretending to be cowboys out in the Great Plains, taming the frontier. Except now, here, far from the frontier, it was better for these men, safer, because the Cheyenne who had been brought here were not allowed any sort of weapons. There was no question of them fighting back. They had no better chance than the deer or the pheasants."

She sipped her lemonade. Elias stared out at the land.

"As he got older," Valeria said, "Augustus grew tired of the difficulties associated with these sorts of hunts, and it was getting more and more expensive for him to hide the truth of what was happening here. He returned to allowing only the hunting of animals. He had grown quite interested in the possibilities of breeding. There were various projects to strengthen species in danger of extinction, and some real success with that, most notably with the bison."

"Yes," Elias said quietly, "I have seen pictures of the bison here. A long time gone."

"The breeding work ended," Valeria said, "when my father, Tiberius, took over. He had no interest in any of the science. The only things in the world he loved were money, hunting, and lying boastfully about his achievements. He even opened the park to the public now and then and tried to turn it into a commercial venture." She chuckled. "Augustus put a stop to *that*. What the massacres had awakened here could not be shared with the world."

Elias never told Valeria that he has known this history his whole life, and that he knows more than any of old Augustus's records reveal. It had been strange to hear the story in her words, to learn how she reconciled shards of fact with family lore and her own experience. Her view, then and now, is not wrong in any meaningful way, but it is incomplete, and it is so warped by her conviction that she and her ancestors were the driving force here that, remembering the conversation now, with a lifetime of experience behind him, Elias lets out a bitter laugh.

From the diary of Dr. Steven Baird:

25 June 2016
Very strange recent days.

On the 15th, a book arrived in my mail that was not sent through the post office. It was in a padded manilla envelope, my name and address on the front, but no postage and no return address. The book was *Wild Life in a Northern Forest* by Aleister Baynes Davis, published in 1928 by The MacMillan Company in New York, a book I looked at a few times at the New York Public Library and at the Boston Athenaeum, but I never dreamed I would own a copy of my own — I've only ever seen a couple come up for sale at book auctions and they sell for thousands of dollars (primarily because of its lavish illustrations rather than its rarity). [...] Davis was a zoologist based originally at the Smithsonian and then later at the Bronx Zoo, and who consulted for Adams Park at the end of the 19th century, probably around 1897 or so, when Tiberius Adams was trying to make the park into a tourist attraction.

As far as I've been able to tell, none of Davis's papers regarding his work at the park have survived — I saw the empty folders in the boxes at the Smithsonian where the papers would be; who removed them and why is a mystery — but he refers to his work there briefly in *Wild Life in a Northern Forest*, describing a "private Eden of large game, exotic wildlife, and more variety of plant species than anywhere else on the American continent" where he "once had the honor of providing advice regarding the care and breeding of animals, though soon I discovered that my particular approach to such things is not to the pleasure of the sons of robber barons. Rumors of human behavior more beastly than that of any of the actual beasts hung heavy in the air of the little towns around the place." Only someone who knew of Adams Park already would have any idea that he was talking about it since the book's actual subject is the Northeast Kingdom of Vermont, where Davis retired. Still, I suspect the book was not well received by Tiberius, Valeria, or Claudius Adams. They certainly could have influenced a publisher like MacMillan, as well as at bookstores and any newspapers or magazines inclined to promote the book. It received a few brief reviews on publication but then effe'tively disappeared.

And now I have my own copy. From whom? How? Why? If I were more paranoid than I am, I would suspect someone of reading this diary. But that would be impossible; it lives only on this computer. I back it up to the cloud automatically, but surely — no, even if I were vastly more paranoid than I am, that someone is hacking into my diary is an idea I would not venture. Perhaps someone knows I am finishing up one project and need a new one, and though my interest in Adams Park may not be generally known, it isn't a secret to various librarians and archivists. The kinds of people who can give away a copy of *Wild Life in a Northern Forest* are, I expect, the kinds of people who would know those librarians and archivists.

Still, to calm my inner conspiracy theorist, I am going to switch to writing in an overexpensive notebook I have been saving for just such a purpose.

Other weirdnesses piled on in the following days — Harris Enderby, my editor at SUNY Press, said they've decided to move the publication date of *Sleepy Hollows* up quite a lot, since apparently some other book had to be canceled or something. He had no details, just said my book will be released in September. That barely leaves time for proofreading! I hemmed and hawed a bit, but he was utterly firm. It must be published as soon as possible. Why? His answer, swathed in a fog of empty words, boiled down to: "Because."

In passing, Harris mentioned that he's going to a conference in August at Dartmouth College, an interdisciplinary conference bringing together geographers, historians, ecologists, and psychologists, and he can get me free registration if I can come up with a brief paper that is in some way about human interactions with the New England landscape, preferably "something like psychogeography." (Apparently, they had somebody on their panel who suddenly can't attend.) I have no idea what psychogeography is, but I said yes. I've always found conference papers to be a good way to play around with ideas, and I am especially interested in the location: if I'm at Dartmouth, I can pretty easily go up to Colton and poke around the outskirts of Adams Park, which I have never had the opportunity to do before.

Then I got an email out of the blue from my old friend and teacher John Gannett, who has retired and just moved to a big new apartment in Providence, which, he says, has a guest suite for visiting scholars. He invited me to come down, said he would be delighted to help me with any projects I might have up my sleeve, and if I need anything at the Providence Athenaeum or John Jay Library at Brown, he would be happy to introduce me to people. I love hearing from John, one of the most devoted scholars I know, but it seems slightly odd to get such an email right now unless I am suffering a terminal case of apophenia. It's like the universe has conspired in recent weeks to try to help me with the Adams Park project. I just wish I knew what that project was....

Once Josiah seemed old enough to take her place, Drusilla said she would prefer not to accompany her father to the mansion's tower again. Elias understood and sympathized. There is much of himself in his daughter. She could do the work well, but it haunted her; she has always felt the weight of ancestry, whereas Josiah has a hardness that Elias knew more in the people who married into the family: his mother, his uncle Wayne, Charlotte, and Drusilla's husband, Howard. It takes a certain hard-headedness to agree to marry a Thornton, a confidence and a stoicism inflecting an undeniable love of spouse, heritage, and land. Such confidence and stoicism burned clear in Josiah from an early age. (Perhaps, Elias muses now, that explains his failure to find a spouse.)

"Josiah can work with me in the tower," Elias said. "But there may be times when you are needed there."

"I know," Drusilla said. "Now and then is fine. I understand the need. But it makes me hate this place."

For all their similarity as people, that sentiment from Drusilla was alien to Elias. He finds no pleasure in entering the tower, and certainly it houses something he could call hateful, but he has never felt hatred for the power there, only awe. And he feels something else, something he only admits to himself in rare, brief moments of absolute, scouring solitude: love.

Josiah was thrilled to gain responsibility for the tower, as at first it seemed to him a great honor. The sense of honor eroded with the years, but the sense of responsibility did not, and even when he was away at college and then graduate school, he came home regularly to fulfill his duties.

From the diary of Dr. Steven Baird:

27 June 2016

First entry in the new notebook. It is strange to write by hand again. I used to take most of my notes by hand, and the majority of what I have for notes on Adams Park are scribbles on yellow legal pads, but almost everything I did for *Sleepy Hollows* was on my laptop. I have somewhat forgotten how to compose sentences with a pen. Nonetheless, it feels good. I had forgotten the simple physical pleasure of a nice fountain pen nib on good paper. (I have so few bourgeois affectations that I hope my occasional obsession with fountain pens may be forgiven.)

Deeply anxious. Lots of odd dreams, quite vivid. I need to get working on this project. It's the only solution to these feelings.

29 June 2016
For the last few nights, I have dreamed versions of the same dream: I am walking through woods and come to a small cabin. From inside the cabin, I hear someone scream. The door opens and a man runs out. He doesn't see me. I see two figures in the cabin. They do not see me, either. The man runs and as I watch him, he is swallowed by the ground. Not quite like quicksand, exactly, but more like the ground rising up and enveloping him. Then I wake.

The dream is unsettling but not really a nightmare. I don't wake from it feeling afraid. It feels somehow matter-of-fact. The dream progresses a little bit more each night, I notice more details, I have more of a sense of continuity. The first night it was just screams and then a man disappearing into a mound of soil. This most recent dream was far more coherent: screams, door opens, I watch the man run past, I see the two figures in the house, I see the ground rise up, I see the man disappear.

What is most unsettling about the dream on reflection is that in the dreaming it is not unsettling at all. Even the screams. It is all somehow an irretrievable past for which I am nothing but a distant witness, and my dream self accepts this in a way that my waking self finds strange and, to be honest, chilling.

———————

Elias had been hunting deer with Josiah and Drusilla when Valeria called him on the radio, its noise scattering any animals within earshot. "Will you have dinner with me tonight?" Valeria asked. "Just yourself, please."

It was a strange request. Certainly, they had had many meals together, but usually if it was dinner, Elias received (via one of Valeria's many anonymous servants) a written invitation a few days beforehand, and the whole family was invited.

When he got to the house, a butler led him to a room on the northern side that he had never visited before, a large, windowless den with wood-paneled walls that once must have been quite an impressive sight, but which now stood faded, dusty, cracked, and bruised. Brass sconces once may have held bulbs but now rested empty and oxidized on the walls. A patchwork of ragged rugs covered the rough wooden floor. Hard white light from inexpensive standing lamps pooled in the center of the room. Old chairs and couches, rotting and eaten by generations of mice, lingered in corners, while a simple wooden table and two chairs waited in the light with Valeria standing nearby as if to guard the silver cloches covering their meals.

"Good evening," Valeria said quietly. Shadows highlighted her cheekbones and hung beneath her eyes. The make-up she wore seemed to have been applied with haste, rendering her face, in the hard light, into a mask.

They sat. Waiters, with impressive inconspicuousness, removed the cloches. "Monkfish," Valeria said. "Brought up from Boston a few hours ago, fresh this morning. Enjoy."

As they ate, Valeria said, "Thank you for coming tonight. I know it was impulsive of me."

"An impulse that leads to monkfish is not an impulse I am going to question," Elias said.

"I will give you some to take home for your family. I am sorry I asked only you up here. But as you can see, I had something in mind."

"This is not a part of the house I've visited before."

"I rarely come here myself," Valeria said. "Augustus used to call it the Den of Iniquity. A joke. But also, not. Until my father's death, the walls were covered with the heads of their trophy animals. And worse trophies, too. The men would sit in here for hours, drinking cognac, smoking cigars, playing cards sometimes, other times discussing ways to carve up the world. As you can see, I have not given the room much attention."

They ate in silence.

"The room," Elias said, "has meaning for you now. To-night."

"Yes." Valeria set her fork and knife on her plate with finality. "I need to remember that my family were not — are not — good people. To our credit, we seldom believed we were. We are people who cherish one thing only, and that is power. I must remember this."

"Why? I mean, why must you remember? There's no reason you can't be better than your ancestors."

Valeria smiled as if she were looking at a particularly stupid child. "I wish that were true. Honestly."

"I don't understand."

"Steven Baird has fallen in love. A nice young man. They seem compatible."

"And this upsets your plans for him."

"Yes. The nice young man distracts him from what *ought* to

be his passions. It will delay things. Or worse."

"So, you are going to intervene."

"Yes."

"But you hesitate."

"I do."

"We are eating in this room now to ... conjure something?"

"Yes. To conjure courage. The courage to wield power."

"I do not think I understand my role in this."

"You are my witness. And sounding board. I trust you. You will, I hope, tell me if I am insane."

Elias raised his eyebrows. "I am no psychiatrist."

"It is not a professional opinion that I seek."

Valeria walked to a bookcase in a dark corner of the room and removed an object. When she brought it to the table, Elias saw that it was a large, dusty glass jar. Inside the jar, suspended in murky liquid, floated a left hand.

"This is the only thing I kept from this room," Valeria said. "The only iniquity I did not return to the land. There was an old label on it. Even then the glue had mostly dried, and it fell off. It said it is the hand of a Cherokee warrior. I did not know at the time why I kept it. It was repulsive to me, nauseating. Ghastly. But I had an intuition that it would be of use."

"Will it be of use?" Elias asked.

"Yes. I will take it to the tower and make an offering."

"Why not take it directly to the cave?"

Valeria coughed out a low chuckle. "There is not enough courage in the entire universe for me to do *that*, Elias."

She returned the jar to the shelf, then rang a small bell near the door. Waiters cleared the table.

"Well," Valeria said. "Am I insane?"

"No more or less than the situation you have found yourself in," Elias said.

Valeria laughed, her amusement seeming to Elias true and unforced. "I could not ask for a better response," she said. She sighed. "And still, the situation weighs on me."

"As it should," Elias said. "The wielding of power is no small thing."

A waiter brought two plates of chocolate cheesecake and placed them on the table.

Valeria said, "I almost brought the jar up to the tower when Lily left. I thought I might use it as an offering then. In exchange for her return."

"Why didn't you?"

"A failure of courage. Or a moment of ... goodness."

"Do you regret that?"

Valeria stabbed the cheesecake with her fork. "Every hour of every day," she said.

From the diary of Dr. Steven Baird:

29 July 2016

Back from Providence. A good visit, and it was pleasant to go to the Athenaeum and the Brown library with John Gannett, though I didn't locate anything of any great use to my research. I have done a good survey, it seems, of available archives, and I expect the next phase ought to be the arduous work of traveling through northern New England to various little town libraries, records offices, and local historical societies, seeking some needle in a haystack, even though I'm not really sure what the needle would look like. Nonetheless, talking to local experts, the carriers of lore, is likely the only way to find what remains hidden, if not lost.

Doing some reading in preparation for the BU environmental history course I got roped into teaching, I was struck by this passage in Richard W. Moore's chapter in At *What Cost? Shaping the Land We Call New Hampshire* (ed. Richard Ober; Concord, NH: 1992):

> The desperate decision of Native Americans to abandon their traditional lands in New Hampshire was influenced by a series of calamities: invasion by the Mohawks, disease, and growing conflict with a burgeoning population of whites. But what ultimately displaced the native population was a concept: the ownership of land. Land that had been used traditionally for centuries was suddenly owned by claim of European thrones and their friends. One of the final ironies of the transition from Native American to English settlement was that Passaconaway, great sagamore of the Pennacooks, had to petition the Massachusetts General Court for a grant of several square miles along the Merrimack below Amoskeag Falls on which to spend his final days. (p. 37)

Hold onto that: *What ultimately displaced the native population was a concept: the ownership of land.* Could be a theme for an entire course. But then I'd probably get fired for being too much of a Marxist.

13 August 2016

Dartmouth conference paper I think is pretty much finished, and it's not as terrible as I expected it would be. The title is cheeky, but I'm sticking with it: "Live Free and Die: Expressions of Individualism and Property in 19th Century New England's Small Burial Plots." Half the information comes from a paper I wrote in grad school, the rest is pretty generic research, but I think it all works okay for what it is.

Got an interesting email from someone at the University of New Hampshire a couple days ago, Gretchen Leroux, a lecturer in history there, who said she was referred to me by John Gannett, as she has been developing an article on Adams Park and has some items I might want to see. I asked John, and he said he's never heard of her, which is weird, but his memory's not what it was, and even in his prime he wasn't very good with names. (But wouldn't he remember referring somebody to me?) She is definitely a lecturer at UNH: she's on their website and her email address is from the university. I found a couple publications in small journals under her name — an article on rural culture, land use, and conservation along the New Hampshire/Vermont border from 1890-1930 and an article on northern New England paper mills and the debate over public lands. It seems she has done some work for the New Hampshire Historical Society and for the Society for the Protection of New Hampshire Forests. Thus, it's entirely possible that she knows about Adams Park and has access to resources I'm not even aware of. Pretty exciting, actually. She's away for a bit, and I've got the conference next week, so we made tentative plans to meet at the UNH library just before fall semester classes start for both of us.

[...]

———————

I t pleases Elias that Valeria told him about Steven Baird's impending visit before she told Josiah. She certainly knows that Josiah is the person who most needs the news, but it was Elias she summoned first. Elias has not been in the tower for a very long time, and the success or failure of Steven Baird as the ancestor who returns depends entirely on how he is received there. That Valeria still trusts Elias and sees him as the head of his family warms him.

He discovers Josiah splitting wood near the farmhouse. "Steven Baird will be visiting the tower soon," Elias says.

Josiah stands still, axe in hand, and stares out at the horizon. "I see."

"Valeria will give you the details. He will probably visit during the day once or twice, then...."

"All right." Josiah takes a deep breath, releases it slowly, hoists his axe, and continues splitting wood.

Later, during a lull in conversation at dinner, Elias says, "Valeria told us today that Steven Baird will be visiting soon."

"Soon?" Drusilla says.

"Within the next two weeks."

"Who is Steven Bear?" little Rachel asks.

"Steven Baird," Drusilla says. "He is a relative of Valeria."

Rachel clearly has no idea what that means, but she nods as if her mother's statement answers every possible question.

Elias turns to Howard. "You know what this means. But you do not need to feel bound to our commitments."

"I knew when I married Drusilla. I knew. I accepted the responsibility then, and I accept it now. This is our family."

They eat their dinner in silence.

From the diary of Dr. Steven Baird:

25 August 2016

Back now from meeting with Gretchen — and will make some notes on that — but somewhere along the way I lost my other notebook — the one with notes from the visit to Colton — all the photos from the trip are gone from my phone — everything from this entire month is gone from my computer. I discovered this as I pulled up stuff on my laptop — tried to pull up stuff — and it was just — *not there.* I showed Gretchen the website of the Dartmouth conference to prove I wasn't lying about being there. It was embarrassing. And terrifying. I know I didn't dream writing 30 pages of notes in my work notebook and also taking at least 50 pictures and typing up a bunch of stuff. But it's *all gone.*

This notebook here will now become my only one, and I will carry it with me and not let it out of my sight until I know I can somehow or other protect the information.

Gretchen said she believed me that I had taken all the notes and photographs. She said there are powerful forces — immense wealth — behind Adams Park, and I should assume they have basically the surveillance and hacking capabilities of a major government organization like the NSA. I laughed when she said it, but she was absolutely serious, and the more I think about it, the more I am beginning to think she might be right to be so serious. As she said, though Adams Park obviously still exists — I saw the gate, I saw the walls, I saw the surveillance cameras — it has not been mentioned in any local, regional, or national press except for three articles (in 1962, 1975, and 1983) about, in the first case, two elk that got out and wandered through the streets of Colton; and, in the second and third case, about neighbors being annoyed by wild boars that escaped from the grounds. For a place that takes up anywhere from 10-50,000 acres (estimates vary wildly) to attract so little attention is just not probable. It's, as she said, a place conspicuously inconspicuous.

But though I like her and she gave me a couple good leads on information, as well as a postcard for the park from 1902 that I had not seen before and a drawing of a hunting cabin next to a lake that an old man told her was made by his father in the 1920s when, as a young man, he did some work helping to clean up after a storm — a cabin that looked familiar, so I must have seen a picture somewhere before — nonetheless, she has the affect of one of those people you see in UFO documentaries who are sure that they know exactly what the aliens are doing. Not that she made any great claims — aside from implying that the park's overseers have super surveillance powers, she didn't claim certainty about anything. It was just her way of speaking, her presentation of herself that made me think she was some sort of fanatic. Which is unjust to her. She said nothing fanatical, really. She did say she suspects the park was used for animal trafficking for a long time and may still today be used for that. They could be raising all manner of animals in there — nobody would know — then selling them to dodgy zoos and to billionaires who want a real rhinosaurus for their kid's birthday party or something. I guess that's plausible, though I do think the locals would have heard something, that they would see trucks at least bringing animals in and out, and all the locals I talked to said that the traffic in and out of the park was sparse and was rather ordinary. So maybe Gretchen is an animal rights activist or something, a covert PETA operative....

I'm just angry about — and painfully perplexed by — the loss of all my notes from the Colton trip. I need to rewrite what I can from memory while it's still relatively fresh in mind. But right now — I need to sleep.

———————

Josiah tells them that Steven Baird's first visit will be a brief one during the day. There might be other brief visits after that, depending on how he seems, depending on what Valeria makes of him. She instructed Josiah to tell his father to be patient. The right time will come.

Josiah asked Elias to climb Gray Mountain with him. He did not explain, but his request seemed urgent. Elias agreed, even as he dreads the long ascent, particularly the rocky escarpment before the peak.

They climb in silence together. Now and then, Josiah points toward a bird in a tree, or Elias stops to examine animal tracks, but they are not men who feel a need for chatter. As the trees diminish and the slope becomes more rugged, they focus on their steps. Josiah is careful to make sure his father climbs slowly, steadily, carefully, pausing for water or to eat some of the nuts, berries, bread, cheese, and jerky they brought. "There is no rush," Josiah says. It is something Elias remembers saying to him many times over the years.

"Never rush a mountain," Elias says.

"A wise man once told me that."

"A wise man or a wise ass?"

"Sometimes they're one and the same," Josiah says. He smiles and gives his father a soft slap on the shoulder.

They pass alongside a ledge, then through a narrow crevice between boulders and up a steep incline around the eastern side of the mountain until they reach the rounded, weather-beaten rock of the summit — the place, Elias used to tell the children, where clouds are born.

They sit atop the sun-warmed rock, catching their breaths and resting their legs, looking out over the vast spread of forest, meadows, lake, all radiant in afternoon light from a clear blue sky. The mansion's mountain, which has no name, stands at the far opposite side of the park, visible only as a small silhouette.

The leaves of a few trees have already changed to the fiery colors of fall. From somewhere below Gray Mountain comes the high, sweet, echoing call of a hermit thrush.

"The wild pigs are strange now," Josiah says. "They keep burrowing into the ground of the sunken lands. I found dozens of them yesterday. I scared them away with a shot, but they didn't go far. I could not see what they were digging for. I don't know if it was purposeful or something else. Vestigial. A recursion. This morning, I found seven pigs that smothered themselves in the ground."

"From here, the land still looks as it always has."

"Yes."

"I was walking along the western side of the lake the other day," Elias says, "and I thought I saw a bison across the shore. Could have just been shadows."

"Did you hear wolves howling last night?" Josiah asks.

"Yes. I assumed it was a dream."

"Perhaps."

"How are the deer?"

"I thought they were skittish last week, but it's something else now. If I didn't know better, I would say they are jubilant."

"It's the same with the elk. They were all over in the west. They've been there for a while now, but yesterday and today, they were venturing farther east than I've seen them go in a long time."

"And the birds. Everywhere. Wild ducks, great blue heron, nighthawks, all the robins, the chickadees, everything."

"Anticipation," Elias says.

They stare out together at the expanse.

From the diary of Dr. Steven Baird:

28 August 2016

Dreams again — vivid in what I can only call a *physical* way — the temperature isn't terrible for August, but it's pretty humid in the city, and the humidity has found its way into my dreams. I don't remember the dream well, just remember a sense of being in a jungle, but it had walls, so maybe a greenhouse, but very big. I was crawling along the ground in dark, wet soil. Vegetation all above. The vegetation moved as if in a regular wind, but there was no wind, just the stifling humidity. Hard to breathe. The vegetation — leaves, vines — brushed against me, as if it was curious about me, but then more than that, somehow — not erotic, though I feel like if I describe it, it will sound like some weird sexual thing — I remember the sensations or the impression of sensations (the dream of a dream of sensation?) — the leaves and vines cradling me, the soil a warm wet bath — but then I woke choking.

6 September 2016

Classes have started (BU and Lesley, including the extra class at BU on environmental history, which caused some ruckus in the department, and Amanda had to get special dispensation for me to teach it, but she assures me it's all fine now, just bureaucracy and territorialism, the twin engines of academia) so I have not had time to continue anything with Adams Park, but for reasons I do not want to put in writing I am certain that my email is being monitored, my postal mail is being read, and my apartment has been searched at least once in the last week. I carry this notebook with me at all times and put it under my pillow as I sleep. This seems both childish and prudent. Also, the dreams continue to be vivid and consistent: humidity, vegetation, connection. They have developed something of an erotic element, or, most likely, I have developed an erotic response to them, which is disturbing.

9 September 2016

In an attempt to alleviate my erotic response to dreams of vegetation, I signed in to Grindr for the first time in many months. And found a guy. He was more aggressive than I thought I wanted, but it ended up being a good thing. I think we are going to meet again.

11 September 2016

Never an easy day, and especially not on the notable anniversaries like this one: 15 years. Can't help but think of Carol and Serena, who were just going for a walk downtown on a beautiful morning. They were the people who first really showed me New York, who welcomed me to the city, kept trying to entice me to Manhattan from Brooklyn (and I kept trying to get them to join me in Park Slope) — and then…. Afterward, I just had to get out. I came up with lots of excuses, remember that one therapist even saying I had PTSD, but I can see the truth now: that I just couldn't imagine — didn't want to imagine — the city without "my girls." So, I went as far away as I could, and thus an academic career began. As a kind of escape. An escape from all that New York meant to me … but an escape into what? I'm not sure it's a question I have asked enough. Certainly, it's not a question for which I have any sort of answer.

15 September 2016
Sleepy Hollows was published today. Even though I wish we had
followed the original schedule and it hadn't been rushed into
print to fill an open slot, I am proud of it. Relieved, even.

Got a nice email from Harris Enderby congratulating me on
the book's release. I suppose it's standard operating procedure
for an editor, but it was nice to hear from him anyway. The
world feels oddly silent. It's strange — you spend all those years
working toward this moment, and then the moment comes, and
... life goes on. Nobody notices. The clock continues to turn.
Traffic keeps moving. Pedestrians in the street don't all come to
a stop and tip their hats to you.

I don't know what I expected. Somehow, in my unconscious
mind, I hoped today might be different from every other day,
that somehow the universe might pause and send some confet-
ti my way, blow a trumpet, crash some lightning. I've honestly
never felt so alone. I hate to say it, but I miss Jesse. I would have
been so embarrassed at the big deal he would have made of the
book, the pride he would feel. I would have poo-pooed it — just
an academic book, nothing to get excited about, nobody will
read it — and he would have told me that for once in my life I
ought to give up being humble, for once in my life to let an accomplishment feel like an accomplishment. He would have said
that, and I might even have allowed myself to listen to him. But
it's not something I can say to myself. And nobody else cares.
My parents are gone, Jesse hates me, all my "friends" at Lesley
and BU are more like acquaintances, and all my friends from
grad school (how many? Three I'm still in contact with once or

twice a year?) are quietly resentful, stuck in the amber of their own frustration at stalled careers.

Thus, alone. But with a book published today with my name on the front cover.

28 September 2016

Everything is terrible. Continued things with Claude from Grindr, which was fun at first, but then he thought I wanted more than I did. I don't blame him. I was attracted to how blustery and aggressive (and yes, violent) he was and.... I hate doing the "it's not you, it's me" thing to him, but when it's true, it's true. I got pretty bruised and lacerated the last time and didn't enjoy it. Not his fault, my not enjoying it. Just me. I get so passive, I dissociate, and I guess that's what I want, but I need to come to grips with the fact that really and truly, most deeply, what I want is to be alone.

Dreams are getting weirder, too, lots of stuff with shadowy men in shadowy rooms, but the vegetation is always out there on the borders, just beyond the walls, as if waiting — sometimes more than waiting, sometimes vines in between cracks in walls, moss growing on old windows and weathered wooden floors. Last night vivid feeling of moss on my feet as I stood there with a shadowy man whose hands slowly, slowly tore my flesh. At least I'm not having a sexual response to it anymore. [...]

My classes are a disaster, and I fully expect not to have at least one contract renewed next term. I am drinking too much. Need to remind myself of that: *I am drinking too much*. I sometimes don't notice and then wonder why I feel like an aching sponge of puss for days. You read it here first. *Quit drinking, quit Grindr, enjoy solitude, get back to work.*

30 September 2016

Called Jesse. Amazingly, he answered the phone. Last time I called, he told me to stop being a stalker and threatened a restraining order. He said it's good I called, he has news: he's engaged to be married to a lovely guy named something I don't remember. He asked if I was well. I said I am. I wanted him to know my book was published. That's what I said, the way I justified myself, even though I found it very difficult to speak. (Hearing his voice again threw me for a loop.) (And engaged. To be *married*. That was fast.) He said he was proud of me. Asked if I'd gotten the therapy we had talked about. I lied and said yes. I lied and said I had some great job prospects and would probably have a full-time position in six months at the most. He sounded actually happy for me. He said he was glad I called, and I think he really was. But when he said goodbye, I also knew it meant goodbye.

17 December 2016

I got careless and left this notebook on the table and got home to find it missing all the entries from October and November.

n the day of Steven Baird's first visit, Elias stays inside the cabin. He considers going down to the sunken lands or walking around the lake, but fear

crawls into him as he feels the new presence arrive. Fear of what, he does not know. His hands shake. Goosebumps rise on his arms. His mouth goes dry, his tongue thick. He sits down on a chair heavily. He wonders if perhaps he is having a heart attack, if perhaps this is the time of his dying, but that is an overreaction. Fear is not something he has felt in a long time. It is unfamiliar to him.

Within the fear, too, he senses something like rage. That is what shook his hands and body. It had been there, hiding, a vein of anger in his nights, especially ever since he first learned of Steven Baird's ancestry, and now the anger seeks some outlet. The man has done nothing wrong; he is the child of a line spawned by an evil act committed by Claudius Adams against a helpless woman who had already suffered greatly, and now that child, as a man, must enter the tower and face the consequences set in motion long before anyone still alive was born. Elias wants to believe there is purpose, even goodness, in the universe, but recognizing its absence is what distinguishes the Thorntons from Valeria Adams, who believes with great certainty that what she has set in motion is revenge — and perhaps justice. But those are human ideas, and if the land taught Elias anything over the years, it is that human ideas have no more substance than a field of morning fog.

Drusilla, Howard, and Rachel come into the house after foraging mushrooms. Elias sits still in his chair.

"Getting cold out there," Howard says.

"Octobers can be cold," Drusilla says. "You okay, dad?"

"I'm okay."

Rachel brings a handful of mushrooms to him. "We found the good mushrooms, granddad. These won't hurt you. We don't like the ones that hurt you."

Elias smiles and takes a mushroom from her little hand. "It's a beauty," he says. He pops it into his mouth. "Tastes good, too."

Rachel cackles with joy.

Later, Josiah returns. He does some pointless work in the garden, then comes in for dinner. Finally, after everyone else has gone to bed, Elias and Josiah stand outside and look up at a wild and starry sky. Only then does Josiah speak of the visitor. "He is a quiet man," he says. "I think Valeria liked him. Yes, I know she did. He seems excited to come back in the future."

Elias nods.

Josiah takes his hand, and then, to the surprise of father and son both, they embrace.

From the diary of Dr. Steven Baird:

3 January 2017

I think I have gotten past the depression that set in after all my teaching contracts were not renewed. The grant from the Hoadley Foundation was both mysterious and lifesaving. Certainly, when I got the letter in October offering me the grant (on Gretchen's recommendation), it was a great relief because I knew I would not be asked to teach anything at BU for the foreseeable future and that my teaching at Lesley was also in jeopardy, but in the midst of everything, I did not realize what a great relief it would be to not have to teach and instead to bury myself in archival research. It was a blow to my ego to be fired — "nonrenewed" is a bloodless way of saying it, and I loathe the bureaucratic euphemism — and a pain to my soul to know that I fully *deserved* to be fired but given everything that happened in October and November it's a miracle I ever showed up for any of my classes at all. I have no doubt a psychiatrist would see my mental state during those months as something like a psychotic break.

Now, having come out the other side of it all, having begun to heal from the wounds to my pride, I can recognize that the Hoadley Foundation, whatever it is, and for whatever reason, is providing me with more money than I would make even on a full-time contract at either BU or Lesley (basically the annual salary of a tenure-track assistant professor; hardly exorbitant but for the first time in my life a living wage), and all I have to do is travel around to libraries and historical societies in search of information about Adams Park, then write a final report of 5-10 pages (more if it seems appropriate). What felt, only a few weeks ago, like the end of my career, now feels like a new beginning.

17 January 2017
Cleaning out my bedroom closet, I found the pages of this note-book from October and November. They were folded up and stuck in a shoebox full of junk (expired ID cards, some birthday cards from Jesse I forgot to throw out, some old receipts that I now don't know why I kept). I have no memory of putting the pages there, but there was nothing to suggest someone else did. Why would somebody other than myself hide my own papers in my own apartment?

It was disappointing to read them because my memory is that despite everything, and with Gretchen's help, I did some good research in the fall. This does not seem to be the case.

Most of what I wrote on those pages was nonsense, long chronicles of strange dreams that I kept trying to do amateur analysis of, attempts at coming up with some sort of cipher that would keep my words from being known by anyone other than myself, ever more paranoid delusions, lists of names with birth and death dates and lots of lines and circles connecting them, etc. Madness.

With a tinge of despair but primarily a triumphant sense of putting the past behind me, I burned the pages in the kitchen sink.

———————

Valeria summons Josiah and Elias to the house for lunch, a simple spread of salad and sandwiches.

"Steven Baird will return tomorrow evening," she says.

"You like him?" Elias says.

"Oh yes," Valeria says, "very much. This time, I hope he will stay."

"We should prepare, then?" Josiah asks.

"Yes," Valeria says. "We should prepare."

From the diary of Dr. Steven Baird:

25 January 2017

Gretchen has disappeared. It is the strangest thing. An email I sent to her bounced back. I assumed it just meant she was not teaching this term at UNH, so I sent a note to the department chair asking if there's another email she uses or some way to get in touch with her. Got a perplexed note back: "I have never heard of that person. Certainly, she has not taught here during my time as chair, including this fall." I looked at the faculty page of the website, which I figured might not have been updated very often (those things tend not to be), and she was not there. I put the address into the Internet Archive and looked at previous versions. None I saw had her on it.

It gets weirder. I Googled her name. Nothing came up. None of her articles, no references to her on the NH Historical Society website or the Society for the Protection of NH Forests website, nothing. I searched JSTOR and Project MUSE and every other database I could think of.

I checked my computer for her emails. There weren't any. None I wrote to her, either.

There are no easy answers to this. The answer that is least disturbing is that I was right to be paranoid about my computer's security, and in fact, somebody hacked both my email account and my browser, creating false web pages. The person I met as "Gretchen" — notably, not at an office but at the café in the library, a public place — could have been an actor, someone trying to find out what I knew and to influence my interpretation of the research.

As unlikely and paranoid as that answer is, it is notably less terrifying to me than the idea that I was, and perhaps still am, completely delusional.

And what of the Hoadley Foundation? I have received the first check from them. My bank account is healthy. Truly. I have the statement right here in front of me. I called the bank to confirm it. The money is real. Yet it was Gretchen who recommended me to the Foundation. Their letter says it. It is now the only place where I have her name on paper, uneraseable.

Though there is little information about the Hoadley Foundation online, there is legal paperwork available confirming their existence (incorporated in Portsmouth, NH) and, to whatever extent legal paperwork is able to do so, their legitimacy.

I think the best thing for me to do is to try not to obsess over anything from the fall, including Gretchen, and to focus on my work. Life is full of anomalies and mysteries. Best to move on. My own past is meaningless. The past I need to concern myself with now is that of Adams Park.

29 January 2017
Dreams of vegetation, soil, humidity returned for the first time in at least a month. I woke painfully aroused.

31 January 2017

I think it makes sense to end this notebook and return to keeping my research organized in my regular manner on my computer. Much as I have enjoyed letting my pen flow, I do not think this journal is providing me with anything other than distraction, and I need now to move past distraction.

[...]

———————

Two hours after Steven Baird's arrival on the night Valeria hopes he will decide to stay on at the estate, Drusilla and Elias wait inside the main entrance of the east wing for Valeria, Josiah, and Steven to make their way there after dinner. A massive round shield with a blue, white, yellow, and green coat of arms dominates the left wall of the small entrance, while a windowed corridor to the right connects the main section of the house. A marble staircase leads from the entrance up around the stone tower that dominates the wing.

Though they have never been prohibited from any area of the house, Drusilla and Elias feel no hurry to ascend to the east wing itself.

As twilight drifts to darkness, the house's automatic lights turn on, and soon Elias hears footsteps and voices. Valeria and Josiah lead Steven Baird in. He is shorter than Elias expected, balding, a bit plump, the middle-aged body of a man who spent most of his day in a chair, his spine curved from years of poring over books and manuscripts, his eyes aided by unfashionably large glasses.

Valeria offers introductions and then, quivering with impatience or excitement or both, dashes up the stairs and pushes open the heavy wooden door to the room at the top of the tower, a large round space that once, long ago, had been lined with leather-bound books and filled with furniture from the castles of Europe and sculptures from ancient Rome.

The books and furniture are still there, somewhere, in the humus and the lichen and the moss. Roots, branches, and leaves burst from the cave directly beneath the east wing and bore through the floors, supplanting inorganic architecture with rhizomatic life. The Roman sculptures now float like ghosts in the flora.

"Take your shoes and socks off," Josiah tells Steven Baird. "They'll get ruined otherwise. Once the place knows your breath, it will be fine, just like walking any other terrain, but for now, you are a stranger."

"The ground is solid," Valeria says, "but also alive. It will welcome you."

Elias remembers his own first step into the room, his father leading him carefully toward the mossy areas of the floor. The room smelled then as it does now, like a forest after summer rainfall. Elias remembers the prickle of the leaves and stems, the tingle as they explored his skin.

Steven Baird does as he was told, clearly confused by what he sees, his face holding the expression of someone uncertain whether he is awake or dreaming. "Oh," he says quietly as he steps into the room. "Oh my," he says, then issues sounds like those of a dove or pigeon. He glances at Elias with panic in his eyes, but that panic soon subsides. The room likes to calm its guests.

"Come," Valeria says, "and meet your ancestor. My grandfather."

They move through the maze of branches and leaves to the center of the room, where a tangle of vines forms a pulsing, nest-like cocoon around what had once been, and in some ways still is, the body of Augustus Adams.

As Steven Baird stands staring, green tendrils climb his legs.

"He likes you," Valeria says. "He is glad you have come home."

"He —" Baird stammers, the vegetal exploration having penetrated, Elias expects, the most intimate parts of his body, "he — is — is in — in pain —"

"Oh yes," Valeria says. "He wants to die. He wants us to let him go." She leans in toward the desiccated skull cradled in green leaves. "But we won't do that, will we, Augustus?" she whispers. "You don't deserve it. No death for you, not yet, not quite. For you, the only possibility is this long, slow, beautiful absorption into the land. A land which hates you."

Speech has been impossible for more than a century (blackberry briars fill the mouth in the skull, spores nestle in the lungs of the body), but Augustus makes his feelings clear through rhythms of life older than any human.

Valeria says, "I will be leaving you, grandfather, but Steven is here now, and he will continue what my father so unwittingly began when he gave you to the cave all those years ago. Do you feel any trace of Tiberius anymore? Or my mother?" To Steven, she says, "Poor Claude disappeared quickly; he was all poison, but my parents held on for a long time, providing far more nourishment than I would have expected."

The room shivers as if a breeze blows through the leaves and vines.

"We should go," Josiah says. "We're agitating things."

The floor shudders with life. A thrumming sound, a dry and hollow moan, echoes from far below, reverberating through the stones of the tower.

Elias has never felt the place so alive. The force of Augustus's despair and hatred require new energy from the structure, rousing the depths beneath their feet.

Outside the room, Steven Baird quietly declines an offer of dinner and says he is feeling tired and still has an hour's drive back to his hotel. Valeria says he is welcome to stay the night, but he clearly wants to leave. Elias suspects Baird is thinking about never returning. He probably has told himself that he will not accept Valeria's offer to take over the estate, not realizing it is too late now. He can go wherever he likes, but he will return in a few days, a week or two at most. The Thorntons know this, Valeria knows this, and Augustus ensures it.

Valeria says goodbye. "The grounds and house are forever open to you," she says, smiling slightly. Josiah then leads Baird down the marble staircase.

"What do you think of him?" Valeria asks Elias and Drusilla as they make their way to the other side of the tower and down narrow granite steps opening on a path to the Thorntons' cabin.

"I haven't seen your grandfather so worked up in a long time," Elias says.

"The man, Baird, seems nice," Drusilla says. "Quiet."

"Bookish," Elias says. "That's probably good, don't you think?"

"Yes," Valeria says. "There were other possible relatives,

here and there, now and then, through the years, but the few who likely had enough blood were too socially connected, too extroverted. It would take them longer to adjust. Steven was the one it seemed least cruel to welcome here. His mother is gone. He has few friends, none of them close. He is happiest alone in an archive."

"And you still plan to leave?" Drusilla says.

"I do," Valeria says. "My grandfather will not last much longer. I want to leave before he does. It feels like the only possible triumph. I'm sure Steven will be back soon, and then I will be free to go. As long as one of us is here, the cave will be satisfied."

Elias does not contradict her, just as his father never contradicted her, nor his grandfather — all the way back to the moment she first entered the cave and thought she understood what she discovered there.

As they walk back to the cabin together, Drusilla asks her father, "Do you think it will be any different when she is gone?"

"Not for a while," Elias says. "Augustus will die. She's right — there is not much left of him now. Your brother is working hard to keep the mansion from being overrun, but I don't think there is any way to succeed at that, especially once Valeria is gone. You know Baird's fate. Nothing we can do about that now. The minute he entered that room... But he should be the end of it. By the time Rachel is old enough to take over for Josiah, I expect things will be more or less as they were before any Adams ever set foot on this land."

"Perhaps not only Rachel. We hope for another in the next year or two."

"That would be nice. The land needs as many of us as it can

get. It's been a while since there were many Thorntons here."

"If Josiah doesn't settle down soon, there won't be any Thorntons at all."

"Godin is a nice name, too. I'm glad it's yours now. Doesn't really matter what the name is. We haven't even been Thorntons for all that long, really."

Howard and Rachel are working together in the kitchen of the cabin to create a salad for dinner from some of the vegetables in the garden beside the farmhouse.

"How'd it go?" Howard asks as Elias and Drusilla walk in.

"About as expected," Drusilla says.

"Mommy, look!" Rachel calls out. She puts a cherry tomato between her teeth, bites down, and squirts red juice all over her face. She laughs uncontrollably.

"I didn't teach her that!" Howard protests.

"I learned it all by myself!" Rachel says between laughs.

Josiah arrives and joins them for a dinner of the salad and some moose stew. Afterward, Drusilla and Howard put Rachel to bed. Josiah also goes to bed, since he needs to get up at dawn to check on a deer herd.

Elias decides to take an evening walk down to the lake.

The night sky is remarkably clear, filled with crystalline stars and a quarter moon bright enough that Elias doesn't need a flashlight to make his way through the forest and across the meadow to the lake. He stands at the shore and listens to the lake breathe quietly against the land. A breeze ripples moonlight over the water. Coyotes howl in the distance.

For a moment, he considers telling his family that they will not follow the command handed down generation after generation, the duty for which they have prepared. They could choose another way. They could, perhaps, lead poor Steven Baird out to the far edge of the forest and let one of the fiercer animals have him — the coyotes, for instance. If Josiah broke Baird's legs and left him, the coyotes might be interested.

Elias lets the idea slip away. As much as he desires another path, this one was set long before his birth, before even Augustus, back to the very first moment when a ship from Europe brought fervent believers to this land, and the believers, knowingly or unknowingly, conjured a spirit of their own fear and vengefulness, one that could not survive except by hiding in a cave and feasting on whatever chaos came its way. Augustus is its perfect instrument: he is its shadow as much as it is his. For as tortured as Augustus might be (desperate to die after all these decades suspended between the material of the land and the spirit of the cave), Elias is sure the force that keeps Augustus alive does so out of something like love. Elias's father had warned him against imagining human emotions in nonhuman things, and Elias dutifully warned his own children of the same. Nonetheless, he cannot help but see it all as a warped love, just as he sees Valeria's abandonment of Lily Davenport as the warping, the calcification, of what had been a true and honest passion.

He kicks a stone into the lake. All of this could have ended when Elias was a toddler if Valeria had simply followed Lily out the front gate. He knows he should not blame her. It has been a great agony in her life, staying behind. As much as he wants to think she had a choice, that the past might have been different, he knows this is not so, prophecy or no prophecy. The cave has always had a special fondness for feasting on Valeria's feelings, particularly her pain, and it never signaled any intention of letting her go. Now, though, it seemed ready for the changes ahead.

Elias kneels at the edge of the water and stares at his moonlit reflection. When did he get so old? His face has more cracks than the mountain ledge. His hair's gone grey and thin. His knees ache. He is not an Adams. Thorntons grow old and die, generation after generation. They take care of the land as they always have, protecting what they can, even in the nightmare years of massacre and slaughter. "Do your best," they always tell their children. "Save what you can. Be ready when the time comes and the blighted family brings their lost one back. That is the day we wait for."

And so, they waited, generation after generation.

And the day has arrived.

Now, they must carry out what they promised to the ancestors. It does not matter that he is a good man, a kind man, innocent. Good, kind, innocent people have been buried throughout this land.

Steven Baird will return. The land recognized him, and the cave sensed him. The moment he drove away from the mountain, he began to yearn. The longer away, the more empty he will feel. The world around him will lose all its attraction, but as he sinks into despair, his mind will fill with images of the place where he needs to be, the place that needs him.

He will return.

Elias stares at the old man's face in the water. Can he do what needs to be done? What his family has prepared so long to do? Yes, of course he can. He has hunted animals all his life, paying them the respect they deserve, feeding himself and his family. This is no different.

He breathes deeply and remembers the words his father taught him, words they recited over and over, and which he taught his own family, and which they will each, even little Rachel, recite again in the morning:

The cycle of life is the cycle of death. In life is our death, in death our life. In our life is the life of the land.

The one who escaped will return.

We will welcome the one who returns.

We will hang him from the door of his house and let his blood spill there.

We will open him from bottom to top.

We will remove the organs and the bladder and the intestines.

We will break the sternum and spread the ribs. We will remove the heart and lungs.

We will cut the skin at the base of the neck. We will pull the skin off.

We will remove the feet, the hands, the head.

We will rinse the body and butcher the meat.

We will crush the bones and grind them to powder. The powder will be spread across the land.

The head and organs will be delivered to the cave where the lonely spirit waits. It will accept the offering and understand that its time in this place is done.

We will live on the meat we have butchered.

The land will have the rest.

The land will have rest.

Notes and Acknowledgements

*C**hanges in the Land* was inspired by the private game preserve established by Austin Corbin (1827-1896) in Sullivan County, New Hampshire, in the late 19th century. Corbin made a fortune in banks, railroads, and real estate. He was a major developer of Coney Island, a place known during his period of ownership as "Sodom by the Sea." He became the president of the Long Island Railroad and joined in a scheme to steal Montauk from the Native Americans, who at that time still had ownership of the land. He owned the Sunnyside Plantation in Arkansas, where he used convict laborers leased to him by the state government to pick cotton. He was a founding member of the American Society for the Suppression of the Jews.

Corbin began collecting animals for hunting on Long Island but soon needed more acreage. Land prices in New Hampshire were low, with many farmers struggling to make a living. Anyone who didn't want to sell their land to Corbin got squeezed out, and soon, he had 20,000 acres or so under his control. He began by stocking the park with animals for his rich friends to come hunt: deer, wild pigs, elk, and bison. He tried various exotic animals, but most died quickly, unable to adapt to New Hampshire's climate.

Corbin died on his New Hampshire estate when he was thrown from a horse, his head smashing against a stone wall. The Corbin family controlled the park until 1944. Teddy Roosevelt visited, as did other presidents, including Grover Cleveland and Woodrow Wilson. In 1908, some bison from Corbin's Park were sent west to help repopulate the western states. A study of the park's fauna (*Wild Life in the Blue Mountain Forest*, 1931) was written by Ernest Harold Baynes, who was appointed as conservator of the park by Austin Corbin, Jr. in 1904. In 1944, the park left the Corbin family's control and was taken over by a consortium of hunters named the Blue Mountain Association. It remains private, open to a small group of wealthy people who want to kill animals.

Aside from a fatal shooting on New Year's Day in 2004, the park rarely enters the news, usually only when some of the wild pigs get through the 26-mile fence and cause havoc in surrounding towns.

Though Adams Park in my story is very much not Corbin's Park, the murderous history of Austin Corbin and the great secrecy around his park did inspire the events herein. Additionally, William Cronin's classic study *Changes in the Land: Indians, Colonists and the Ecology of New England* was often on my mind while writing. American history is a horror story.

I am pleased that a tale of deep histories has been shepherded into this world by three friends I've known for a long time now. Richard Scott Larson read draft after draft of this story as I tried to figure out what it wanted to be — his faith kept me plugging away at an ever more unwieldy manuscript.

For years, I have dreamed that my old grad school office-mate Jeremy John Parker might design a book I'd written, and now he has, exceeding even my greatest hopes for the wonder he could create.

Steve Berman of Lethe Press has been a supporter of my work for many years and, finally, we found a project to work on together. My shelves are filled with Lethe books, and it is a true honor to have one of them now be my own.

This book was written in Plymouth, New Hampshire, a name imposed on N'dakinna, the traditional ancestral homeland of the Abenaki, Pennacook, and Wabanaki Peoples past and present. They remain on the land, and I hope it will be returned to them one day.

—November 2023

About the Author

Matthew Cheney's books include *Blood: Stories, The Last Vanishing Man, Modernist Crisis and the Pedagogy of Form*, and *About That Life: Barry Lopez and the Art of Community*. His work has appeared in *Wilde Stories, Best Gay Stories, Weird Tales, Conjunctions, One Story, Nightmare Magazine, The Dark, LA Review of Books*, and *Woolf Studies Annual*. His story "Blood" was recently adapted as a film titled *Jill*, starring Tom Pelphrey. He lives in New Hampshire.

About the Typefaces

This book is typeset in IM Fell Double Pica, a modern revival font based on The Fell Types which take their name from John Fell, a Bishop of Oxford in the seventeenth-century. The original typecase was cut by Peter de Walpergen in 1684 then digitally reproduced by Igino Marini, an Italian civil engineer, starting in the year 2000.

The drop caps are set in Daemonesque, designed by Graham Meade, a prolific Australian type designer from Clayton, South Melbourne.